This igloo book belongs to:

....

igloobooks

Written by Stephanie Moss
Illustrated by Francesca De Luca

Designed by Alice Dainty
Edited by Claire Mowat

Copyright © 2020 Igloo Books Ltd

An imprint of Igloo Books Group,
part of Bonnier Books UK
bonnierbooks.co.uk

Published in 2020
by Igloo Books Ltd, Cottage Farm
Sywell, NN6 0BJ
All rights reserved, including the right of reproduction
in whole or in part in any form.

Manufactured in China. 0920 001
10 9 8 7 6 5 4 3 2 1

Library of Congress Cataloging-in-Publication
Data is available upon request.

ISBN 978-1-83903-731-3
IglooBooks.com
bonnierbooks.co.uk

FARM STORIES

igloobooks

Contents

Best Farm Friends

Hen and Duck were best friends. They did everything together, except on hot, sunny days when Duck loved to dive into the pond.

SPLASH!

But Hen just stood on the bank, sadly.

I can't swim,

she told everyone.

The other animals giggled and, every time, Duck felt bad for his friend. Then one day, he had a great idea.

Wait here, Hen!

Everyone gathered around the barn. There were all sorts of funny noises coming from inside.

CRASH!
BANG!
CLATTER!

Then, the doors creaked open.

Surprise! I've made you a boat!

8

Hen was so happy, she shook her
tail feathers and helped Duck
take the little boat down to the water.

Jump in! Now we
can play in the water
together all day.

They rowed around and around until they were dizzy, and soon, the other animals wanted to join in, too! First they took turns diving off the side.

SPLISH!

SPLASH!

Then Hen showed everyone how to water-ski.

We're sorry we laughed. You're always welcome in the pond!

Thanks for helping me, Duck. You're the best friend ever!

Chick Learns A Lesson

Chick and Mommy were visiting Horse in the meadow near the woods.

Mommy, what are the woods like?

Mommy told her all about the beautiful flowers and the animals that lived there.

You must never go there by yourself,

said Mommy, but that just made Chick more curious!

When Mommy wasn't looking, Chick took a tiny step toward the woods.

Nothing bad happened, so she took another.

Just like Mommy said, there were little streams and pretty flowers everywhere. Bunnies **hopped** and squirrels **scampered.** They played chase and hide-and-seek all day.

The woods aren't scary at all.

Soon Chick felt sleepy, so she snuggled
down for a nap in the warm afternoon sun.

When she woke up, the sun had
gone down and there were
scary shadows everywhere.

Then Chick heard a voice.

Are you lost?

it asked.

Fox appeared from the shadows, grinning with his sharp, shiny teeth. Chick felt very afraid.

Mommy was right. The woods are really scary!

Then she heard a **SQUAWK!** Mommy had come to find her.

No, thank you,
Fox. I'll take
Chick home.

Little Chick learned a big lesson that day!

Hee-Haw Henry

Henry lived with the horses on Sugarlump Farm.
They all had shiny coats and looked so strong as they galloped along.
CLIP-CLOP! Henry watched them from the field. **HEE-HAW!**

SUGARLUMP FARM

I wish I were special.

The fastest horse of all was Jet.
He loved showing how high he could jump.

The other horses soon had enough of Jet's boasting,
so they trotted far away to graze.

Only Henry stayed.

Watch this!

Henry looked on, cheering in amazement. **HEE-HAW!**
Suddenly. . .

SPLAT!

Jet landed in a deep puddle of gooey mud.

Help, I'm stuck!

cried Jet, looking very worried.

I can't! I'm not strong enough.

Then, Henry realized there was something he could do that none of the horses could.

Henry took a deep breath and. . .

HEE-HAW!

HEE-HAW!

He called and yelled until, finally,
the other horses galloped
across the field.

Fetch some rope. We need to pull out Jet.

The horses tried to pull Jet out, but it was no use.

Henry joined in and pulled as hard as he could. At last, Jet was free!

Little Horse's Big Day

Little Horse wanted to go and play with the farm animals for the first time, but Mommy said she needed someone to go with her.

She trotted over to the henhouse.

They look like
a lot of fun!

But the hens were so busy squawking at each other as they
ate their breakfast, they didn't even notice Little Horse.

So Little Horse galloped through the field
to say good morning to the fluffy sheep.

But the flock herded around her in a circle
until she felt quite dizzy. **BAA-BAA!**

She decided to visit the goats instead, but they were having some sort of strange competition.

One flung himself into a huge puddle and mud went all over Little Horse. **SPLAT!**

YUCK!

she cried.

Then, the cows barged past on their way back from milking.
Poor Little Horse was ready to give up.

No one wants to play with me.

Little Horse felt sad and went home to Mommy.

They were just a bit busy. Let me show you around!

The animals **clucked, mooed, baaed,** and **cheeped.**

We're sorry. Let's go and have some fun!

Sheep's Secret

Whenever Sheep was on her own,
she loved to sing as loudly as she could.

TRA-LA-BAAAA!

No one else had ever heard her until, one day, a mole popped up.

Sheep's cheeks turned bright red.

Please don't tell anyone. I'd be so embarrassed.

Don't worry. Your secret's safe with me.

Then he dived back underground.

The very same thing happened when Mole found Horse sneaking apples from the goat pen. . .

. . . Pig enjoying a quiet bubble bath in the pond. . .

. . . and Bunny nibbling on Farmer Kate's flowers.

The next day, Sheep was in the middle of a secret performance. She stopped when she saw Horse coming. But still he said,

I didn't know you liked singing.

33

Sheep realized Mole must have told Horse her secret, and it wasn't long before everyone else's were out, too!

Let's teach Mole a lesson.

So they waited until Mole appeared from below

34

The Goat Escape

Little Goat had always wondered what was out in the big, wide world.

So he went to explore the field on his own,
when he found that the gate was open!

Little Goat sneaked out and was
about to take a big **SLURP**
of water from a trough.

Suddenly. . .

. . . BOOM,
BOOM!

bellowed a huge bull.

Quick as a flash, Little Goat scrambled away through the fence.

Then he skipped across the field until his stomach started rumbling.

Little Goat snuffled around
for a tasty treat and found
a pile of crunchy acorns.

Just as he was about
to nibble one, he heard
CHITTER-CHATTERING!

THOSE ARE
OURS!

cried two
angry squirrels.

The squirrels **snatched** the acorns, so Little Goat looked for somewhere to have a nap. Suddenly, he spotted two little eyes and a long nose.

This is my den,

said a sly fox.

Ahhh!

cried Little Goat.

He raced all the way back to the farm and
everyone was **very** happy to see him.

Little Goat remembered how much he loved his life
on the farm and he **never** ran away again.

First they ran a race.

Ready, steady, **GO!**

shouted Cow.

Horse **galloped** ahead, with Sheep not far behind.
But Mouse's little legs soon got tired.

Here, let me help.

Horse was in charge of the obstacle course. Goat **darted** over the
hay bales, troughs, and milk-pail towers **faster** than anyone,
while Hen **flapped** her wings and flew across them.

SQUAWK!

Pig thought the obstacles were a bit too high
and trotted around them instead.

No cheating!

called Horse from
the finish line.

Then Duck had a great idea for the next event.

All the animals headed over to the pond
for a swimming race.

I'll be
the judge,

said Cat, refusing
to get wet.

SPLISH, SPLASH! they went, and Duck and Dog tied for first.

Finally, Cow put the animals into two teams.

It's time for tug-of-war!

They all pulled as
hard as they could, but
neither team budged.
Then, Mouse gave an
extra-hard tug. . .

. . . SNAP!

The rope broke and the animals tumbled into a heap
on the ground, laughing and giggling.

It's a
draw!

cried Cow.

This had been the best sports day **ever**.